CURT MOELLER

MODERN FABLES

By Curt Moeller

CURT MOELLER

About the author

Curt Moeller was born in Canada, and has travelled much of the world, living at various times in Japan, Holland, and the UK. He currently resides in Toronto. Modern Fables is his first book.

CURT MOELLER

"Myth is at the beginning of literature, and also at its end."

~Jorge Luis Borges

Table of Contents

CURT MOELLER

I. The Rabbits

Mr. And Mrs. Rabbit were sitting in their home, enjoying a nice meal, when they heard a knock at the door. It was an acquaintance of Mr. Rabbit's who said he was passing through town. "Come in," said Mr. Rabbit, "I'm sure my wife has made enough for dinner for you to join us."

"Much obliged," said the out-of-town rabbit, and Mr. Rabbit took him into the dining room and introduced him to Mrs. Rabbit.

They ate a fine supper of fresh vegetables, and afterwards Mrs. Rabbit went into the kitchen to clean up. The two males, left alone, began to talk about sex, as two male rabbits inevitably will when they're left alone. They spoke of famous bunnies they found attractive, of the virtues of older bunnies versus younger bunnies, and of what was good and bad about the different colours of bunnies ("polka-dotted girls will eat you out of house and home"). Eventually the out-of-towner confessed that, for some reason, he was no longer capable of having sex. "The one I really feel bad for is my wife" he said, and Mr. Rabbit acknowledged that that would be a rotten thing for a female rabbit to endure.

"Listen," the out-of-towner said, "I know this'll sound strange, but would you be willing to go and lay with my wife? She's at a hotel nearby."

"I couldn't" said Mr. Rabbit.

"I understand if you don't feel comfortable, I know it's strange. But you're just the kind of rabbit she likes."

Mrs. Rabbit came into the room just then, and they immediately pretended they had been talking about something else. "I'm going to bed" she said, "I'm tired." Mr. Rabbit gave her a kiss, and off she went.

"Are you sure you won't do it? I know it's strange, but it'd mean a lot to her, and to me too. And I know she'd like you. What do you say?"

"I just don't think I could."

"It's really nearby, and your wife's already asleep. I'll wait here for you. I really would appreciate it."

After some thought Mr. Rabbit agreed to go, and the out-of-towner gave directions to the hotel and the room number. "When you get there, just go into the room and climb into bed."

When Mr. Rabbit got to the hotel, he found the door to the room unlocked. He crawled into bed and began to stroke the soft fur and inhale the sweet perfume of the lovely creature. Within moments he was overcome by lust. When it was over, she rolled onto her side and said "leave the money on the side-table."

"What do you mean?" he asked.

"Over there" she said, pointing vaguely, "on the side-table."

"But your husband didn't say anything about me paying you."

"My husband?" she laughed. "Do you think I'd be in this line of work if I had a husband?"

Mr. Rabbit hastily left some money and ran out the door. He felt the need to get home quickly, but he knew he had to stop at the creek first to wash. Rabbits have an excellent sense of smell, and surely his wife would smell the perfume on him. He washed himself thoroughly, and ran home.

When he got home he noticed the out-of-towner was gone. Confused and exhausted by his evening, Mr. Rabbit quietly tip-toed into the bedroom and got into bed next to his wife, who was sleeping deeply.

His nose began to twitch violently: the scent of the out-of-towner was everywhere!

II. The Horse and the Donkey

One day two friends were playing in a field: one was named Horse, and the other was named Donkey. They were good friends and played together every day, running, jumping, splashing in the water of nearby rivers. They would often race over long distances, but neither was upset by defeat, nor overly pleased with victory: they simply looked forward to the next day's race, and the thrill of speeding along again.

On this particular day however, their race came to an abrupt end. As they were running, with Donkey in the lead by the slimmest of margins, they found themselves entangled, and however hard they struggled, they could not free themselves. The creatures that captured them seemed small, slow, and weak, but were able to use their superior numbers to advantage. Eventually these strange creatures that walked on only two legs managed to bring Horse and Donkey to where they lived, and put them inside a circle of wood that was too high for Horse and Donkey to jump over. For the first time in their lives, Horse and Donkey were held captive.

During the following days, the small creatures tried to get Horse and Donkey to pull heavy objects behind them. Both refused and were beaten for it. This went on for some time, and as the beatings became worse, Donkey eventually gave in, and pulled the heavy object. He was rewarded with food, and was relieved to avoid another beating. Horse, however, refused to do what the small creatures wanted, and continued to take the punishment.

"I think you should just do what they want," Donkey said.

"Why should I?" asked Horse. "I have done nothing wrong to these creatures, nor have they done anything good to me. I owe them nothing, yet they keep me in this small space."

"I owe them nothing either," said Donkey, "but I did what they wanted, and they gave me food, and even better, spared me another beating. That, I think, is reason enough."

"Never," said Horse.

Things continued in much the same way for the next days. Donkey pulled the heavy loads that the small creatures tied to him, and they fed him. Each day the load got heavier, and the small creatures were more demanding that he walk in a straight line, or turn when they pulled him, but his beatings were very slight. Horse continued to refuse, and was beaten worse with each passing day.

"Please, do what they want, my friend, or you will soon die," Donkey said. "You haven't eaten for a long time, and your back is covered in blood. It is a terrible sight. Yes, it is very difficult to pull for them, and I am exhausted, but I am alive, and will continue to be. Please, my friend."

Horse smiled at his friend and in a faint voice said: "perhaps my back is covered in blood, but yours is starting to bend in the middle." They both laughed at this, though neither knew why.

The next day the small creatures came again, and some of them took Donkey, and saddled him with the heaviest load yet, and he dutifully pulled it back and forth, in perfectly straight lines, struggling mightily against the weight. Some of the other small creatures then did something unexpected- they gave Horse some food. Horse ate it up swiftly, but with suspicion. Then one of the small creatures slowly, gently, climbed onto Horse's back. Horse was surprised, and began to run around the circle of wood that contained him, but the small creature held on tight.

The following morning, Donkey was wearily led out of the circle to begin another long day of hauling.

Horse was fed again, and again one of the small creatures mounted his back, and Horse ran in circles. That night, an exhausted Donkey asked: "why do you allow them to sit on your back, but you won't pull for them?"

"They have compromised," said Horse, "so I will compromise."

Life continued like this through the passing of several seasons for Horse and Donkey, with one bearing a heavy load, and the other a light rider. Eventually the small creatures moved them to a much larger circle of wood, and the two were very happy, because they now had plenty of room to run and play as they had before.

"Come," said Horse, "we may not be free as we once were, but at least we can enjoy ourselves. Let's race as we did a long time ago."

Donkey was extremely tired, and had no desire to race, but he could see the excitement in his friend's eyes, and did not want to disappoint him. And so they raced. As Horse galloped along he noticed that he could not hear his friend behind him, and looked back. Horse was surprised to see Donkey so far behind, running without his former speed and grace. So far behind that in fact, it was not actually a race. Horse felt great pity for his friend.

CURT MOELLER

III. The Cat and the Mice

The Mice lived safely and happily in their home. Built beneath two large rocks with a little opening between, their home was impervious to predators because anything small enough to fit through the small portal posed no real threat to them. Outside, however, the Mice took great care to avoid any creature that could harm them. Yet, being mischievous, they enjoyed teasing and tormenting animals that could not harm them. Their favourite victim was the Cat.

Every day the Mice would seek out the Cat, sneak up behind him, and sink their teeth into his tail. Now, it is true that the Cat had sharp teeth, and so if he caught the Mice he could hurt them, but he moved his heavy paws slowly and awkwardly and had never caught any of the Mice before. Day after day, the Mice would creep up, so very silently, behind the Cat, bite his tail, and then scurry in every direction.

'Owwww!' the Cat would shriek, and frantically try to trap them with his paws.

'Ha ha ha,' the Mice would laugh, 'are those love-taps meant to hurt us? No wonder you're so slow, with those giant toe-nails!' Indeed, the Cat did have extremely long, thick toe-nails that slowed him down considerably and made his limbs cumbersome. The Mice would then run back to their home beneath the rocks, leaving the chasing the Cat far behind.

The Cat was known for his patience, so he managed to endure this torment a great deal longer than other animals might have. One day, as he tried to avoid the area where the Mice usually bothered him, he felt a sharp stinging in his tail. He turned to see a group of giggling Mice, and he angrily tried to bite one.

'You'll never catch us,' the Mice taunted him, and they ran towards home. Furious, Cat began to follow, and the Mice even slowed down at times, to allow Cat to catch up and maintain his pursuit.

'You'll never catch us,' the Mice laughed, 'not with those big white toe-nails dragging on the ground!' When they got to the two big rocks they lived beneath, the mice leapt through the small opening, and continued to shout insults at the Cat.

Burning with rage, the Cat lost all of his famed patience, and pawed at the rocks for hours, the jeering Mice spurring him on, swinging his giant toenails savagely until his paws were bloody, and the pain and the fruitlessness of his endeavour forced him to stop.

The Mice did not see the Cat the next day, or the next, or the one after that. But they did see him again, and after several days' absence they were eager to renew their games. They crept up quietly and bit his tail, and the Cat pounced. He swatted one of the Mice and it went flying far through the air. The Cat then chased down and killed two more, pinning them beneath his lean and sharp new claws that had been honed on the entranceway of the Mice's home.

IV. The Frog and the Fish

The Frog lived in the damp, reedy area next to the river, and he spent most of his time there. Sometimes he would venture away from the river to explore inland, but never very far. At other times he would swim in the river, in the stillest parts.

On occasion, when he was swimming, Frog would meet the Fish, and they would exchange greetings, but this was usually brief. One day, while the Frog was swimming, the Fish came up and said 'hello there.'

'Hi.'

'How is everything on land these days Frog?'

'Fine.'

'Good, good,' said the Fish. 'So, nothing special there? On land I mean. Nothing new, I should say. Just the same old day-to-day stuff then?'

The Frog noticed the tone of the Fish's questions and felt playful. 'No, no, Fish,' he said, 'just the same old thing. You know, dragon wrestling, unicorn races, playing with dinosaurs, listening to faerie music, riding on winged-horses. Sure, everything's great on land, but all of that fantastic stuff can get boring after such a long time. That's why I come to the river from time to time.'

'Oh, I see,' said the Fish.

'Sure, why, just the other day some fish friends and I were watching a wizard make ice-fires, when I said to-.'

'I'm sorry, did you say fish?'

'Yes.'

'Fish? On land?'

'Yes, of course.'

'But how?'

'Do you mean to tell me that you don't know?'

'No, no, please tell me!'

'Well, all you have to do is go there, there isn't much to tell.'

'But fish can't live out of water. We can't breathe in the air.'

'Well, not around here you can't, of course. The air is so foul around this filthy river. You just have to go a little further inland and then you'll be fine. You really didn't know that?'

"No,' the Fish said, and then went quiet. After a few moments he asked: 'Do you think I could do it?'

'Do what?'

'Go onto the land?'

'Of course, don't be so cowardly. Just jump as far

inland as you can, and that'll be enough to breathe, although it might take you a few minutes to get used to walking. Apparently it takes most fish a moment to adjust, or so they've told me.'

The Fish was extremely excited. He had always thought of the world as having two distinct parts, and only a few lucky creatures, like frogs, could live in both, but now he too could go onto the land and see for himself all the mysterious things that existed there.

'I'm going,' said the Fish. The Frog congratulated him, and said he'd watch from the shore. The sight of the Frog leaping out of the water gave the Fish confidence.

The Fish swam in a circle a few times, building up speed, and then he charged towards the shore as fast as he could, and threw his body out of the water, flying in a great arc until landing on the ground, quite a distance from the river.

He wasn't surprised that he couldn't walk yet, the Frog had warned him of that, but he was surprised that he couldn't breathe. But the Fish just figured that he wasn't far enough inland yet, and he flipped his body about, moving a little further each time, and he never panicked in those last moments before he died, and he never heard the Frog laughing at him.

V. The Fly and the Chrysalis

A Fly was buzzing around a tree, stopping here and there to eat, to rest, to look at his surroundings. The Fly noticed something wriggling on a branch nearby, and flew over to have a look.

When he arrived at the branch the Fly saw a Chrysalis, moving its tail to and fro. The Fly watched it moving thus for a long time. "What a sad and pitiable creature" said the Fly. "While I can buzz about over the ground and scavenge for bits of food, and if I wish ascend the highest tree. I have a short but glorious life. But you are nothing but a worm in a tree, stuck in spot, and barely able to move. One could hardly call you alive. You're quite disgusting." The Fly laughed, and buzzed away.

The Fly avoided that branch when he flew around the tree the next few days. One day he buzzed a bit closer than he meant to and saw that the Chrysalis was completely dried up. He landed on the branch to take a closer look. He could see that it was just a dry shell, and that it was empty inside. The Fly looked upward when a shadow passed over his head.

Above him, the Fly saw the Monarch, bright in colour and huge of wing. The Fly watched her float in the air musically, sometimes seeming to be blown by the wind, other times appearing to be the conductor of the wind, always with such a natural manner that her movements carried the moral weight of the universe. As the Monarch traced elegant shapes above his head, the Fly fell into a swoon of love for her.

He went towards her, buzzing in a zigzag pattern across the sky. As he got closer he saw the Monarch joining others, and she and her friends conducted the wind in unison. It was a sight too beautiful for his mind to fathom, and he felt dizzy and confused, but he continued onward. He buzzed through the Monarchs once, turned and did the same again. He couldn't slow himself in the air to stop and talk, so each time he passed he whizzed past her unnoticed, as she floated in harmony.

The Fly was so in love with the Monarch that he buzzed back and forth, to and fro, for longer than he had ever remained in the air, refusing to accept that he was unable to speak to her, or even get her to notice him. He continued flying back and forth, so dizzy and confused that he didn't notice himself falling, didn't notice that his wings were no longer buzzing; only noticing the gentle flutter of her colourful wings.

VI. The Ants

In the year 23, all Ants took trains to work, and they had been doing so for a long time. Upon arriving at their worksites, the Ants quickly and enthusiastically began their labour. Large groups of Ants worked together swiftly, efficiently, and effectively, in a spirit of unity, harmony, and selflessness that many other species studied and attempted to replicate- with varying degrees of success, but never with more than a fraction of the collective spirit that the Ants displayed. During the commutes to and from work, the carriages were busy and crowded, and the trains frequently broke down for long stretches of time with the trapped passengers anxiously waiting to be on their way again. The usually even-keeled Ants would at times get aggressive and violent with each other, fighting for a seat, or even just for an extra bit of space. During the commute was the only time anyone could recall Ants ever behaving in such a way. At home in the evenings, Ants would often discuss the incidents of violence, and would recall with nostalgia a time when those incidents were less, when the trains had more seats, were not so crowded, and broke down less often.

In the year 24, the number of incidents of Ants biting off and eating the heads of other Ants increased from 0.8 incidents per thousand citizens in the previous year, to 2.6 incidents per thousand citizens. The number of violent events on the trains more than tripling became very big news in the Ant world, and it dominated the media outlets, with each new occurrence shown repeatedly until it was bumped by the next occurrence. Fear and panic spread.

In the year 25, a new trend emerged. Some Ants (not a great number, but some) would ingest a slow-dissolving poison in the morning before their commute, which stayed in the system for about a day before killing the one who took it. When one commuter bit another's head off and ate it, that act sometimes meant unknowingly ingesting the poison as well, dooming the biter to inevitable demise, and in this way many biting attacks became double homicides. Those that took the poison in the morning but didn't get their heads bitten off on the commute to or from work, survived the day and spent the evening knowing that their time was nearly up. An interesting and perhaps slightly peculiar element of this self-poisoning trend was that those who took the poison never left suicide notes or any explanation for their actions, nor told anyone they had taken the poison and would soon die. Most reached their end mid-meal at the dinner table. Ants eyed each other on the trains more suspiciously than ever after this new trend emerged.

In the year 26, the number of violent incidents on trains drastically reduced to 1.3 incidents per thousand citizens. Some media outlets questioned the government's statistics; while others spoke of a collective denial so strong that sometimes nobody saw the attacks occurring right before their eyes; still others in the media claimed that there were no attacks, and there never had been, and it was all an elaborate ruse to spur investment in infrastructure. The Ants were aware that attacks were still occurring daily, but they could also tell that there had indeed been a decrease in violent incidents. They no longer spoke about any of it at home: fear and panic were now joined by their ally, confusion.

In the year 27, the government installed additional seating along the back walls of the train carriages, and refurbished the train engines to reduce the number of break downs. Violent incidents on trains decreased to 0.8 per thousand citizens that year.

CURT MOELLER

VII. The Lion, the Bull, and the Goat

The Lion was chasing the Bull, and gaining ground quickly. The Bull caught up to his herd, and together they charged the Lion, pushing him back. The Lion kept a distance, but continued to follow.

The herd knew that he was following, and the Lion knew that they knew. He kept his distance, but he continued to follow.

The next day, near dusk, the Bull was at the rear of the herd on the edge of a steep drop. The Lion raced forward, and the Bull panicked and scrambled, causing him to slide down the hill. The Bull rolled a few times on his way down, but somehow landed on his feet and staggered away. The Lion had no wish to fall, and stepped cautiously down the steep hill.

The Bull noticed a cave, and ran into it. The cave was deep, and the Bull went to the farthest, darkest recesses, until he felt a sharp poke in his backside. He was poked a few times before he could discern anything in the darkness, but as his eyes adjusted to the lack of light he could see that it was a goat with short horns, ramming him from behind. The Bull was filled with rage, and wanted to tear the goat into pieces with his horns and hooves, but he knew the Lion was nearby, and was terrified to make any noise. "Please stop that," said the Bull, "I don't want to fight."

"Bulls always attack goats, I'm no fool. I'm only defending myself!"

"Please," said the Bull, "I have no wish to fight you, I am trying to keep quiet. I am hiding from a Lion that was chasing me, and if you know anything about Lions, then you will want to keep quiet too. Let's be friends, we can help each other." The Goat said nothing at first, and only stared at the Bull.

"I understand," said the Goat, "I have seen the Lion, and know he is fierce. But I also know that he never enters this cave, and I know how to watch unseen. If you stick your giant head out to look you can be seen from any distance. We will be friends Bull. I will help you. Now be quiet and don't move. I'm going to keep watch. I'll keep us both safe. And later you can help me too."

"Oh, thank you, thank you," said the Bull, "yes, I can help you later."

"Well, well, well," thought the Goat, "you who hurts my people so often, you who ran into this cave after I was already here and brought the deadly Lion in pursuit, you who is in trouble and needs my help, you who is scared for his life, now you will owe me and pay your debt, and I will keep you as my tool. The other goats will never be able to stand up to me with you at my side. I will be king!"

The Goat was of course very afraid of the Lion, so he watched quietly and cautiously for a long time, until he saw the Lion at a distance, going in the other direction. "He's leaving," said the Goat, "we can go out now. It's safe for us."

As they left the cave, the Goat took the lead, which was only natural since he was the one who had handled the situation with the Lion, the one who had protected them and kept them safe; he was the boss. As they walked out of the cave, the Bull behind and the Goat in front, the Bull began to feel ashamed, he began to resent the Goat, he began to resent himself for running and hiding and letting the Goat keep him safe. As he walked behind, he watched the Goat's small testes dangling down, swinging side to side as he walked. "How dare that little animal with its little balls attack me, and then negotiate to be equals. How dare he…" the Bull snorted as he thrust his horns forward, the right horn tearing both of the Goat's testicles clean off.

The Bull had never heard a sound as loud, as piercing, or as ear-splitting before, for a goat relieved of its testicles does not go quietly. Nor had the Lion ever heard such a sound. The Lion came running from the bottom of the hill to investigate, finding small game, almost dead already from blood loss, and big game, frozen in place with fear of the Lion.

CURT MOELLER

VIII. The Ass and the Mule

I t was a cloudy, foggy, damp day in the mountains, and the Ass and the Mule were each carrying heavy burdens up and down very steep ascents and descents. Both the Ass and the Mule were tired, and wary of the treacherous marching, but the two-legged creature that walked behind them, light of feet with no burden to carry, would not let them stop to rest, nor let them change their route away from the steep mountains.

It was the first time the Ass had been in the mountains, and she lost her footing a few times, and almost fell sideways off a cliff more than once. The Mule, also very tired, had a lot of experience in the mountains and was able to keep her footing, albeit with great effort, and not slip.

"My friend," the Ass said, "I've almost fallen a few times. The load is too much for me to bear, and I feel as though I cannot continue for much longer." The Mule didn't respond.

The trek continued for a long time, up and down, over mossy stones, loose soil, and narrow ledges, as they slowly passed the peaks of each mountain. The

Ass and the Mule took no notice of their surroundings, only looking down at the next place to step along that dangerous route. Whenever they tried to stop due to fatigue, the two-legged creature gave them a whip along the backside.

"I will not last much longer," said the Ass. "Each step is more painful and unsteady than the last. I have only one hope, but I am too ashamed to ask. No, no, not too ashamed to ask. Yes, I am ashamed, but I am also fearful of death. Please my friend, you look so steady and sure on your feet, please take some of my load. With less weight I would be surer on my feet. If you agreed to take half of it, I'm sure we could both survive. Not all of it of course, just half, or close to half, I'm certain that would be enough." Again, the Mule didn't respond, and continued to walk with tired but steady steps.

After another while of walking, the Ass spoke again: "I am sorry that I made that request my friend. I know that you too bear a heavy burden, and that your curse is the same as mine. It was wrong of me to ask you. I know that I won't be able to go much further, and that will be my end. But I believe that you will make it out of these mountains and survive, and knowing that makes my own bleak future easier to accept." The Mule looked quickly at the Ass, but didn't respond.

The march continued for countless more steps, each animal struggling mightily, when the Ass slipped on a wet rock, and tumbled forward. The weight piled on top of the Ass's back fell forward onto her head, breaking her neck and killing her instantly. The Mule and the two-legged creature both stopped and stood silently.

The two-legged creature took all that had been strapped to the back of the Ass, and added it to the back of the Mule. Her double load was now piled so very high and so very wide, that she looked almost like an afterthought attached to the bottom of the great pile. The two creatures, one with two legs and no burden, the other with four legs and a colossal burden, walked on and on through the mountains. The Mule was able to continue for a long time before the burden became too much even for her strong back and legs, and she sank first to two knees, then four, then flat on the ground. She wheezed and gasped, with no chance of ever returning to her feet, while the two-legged creature impotently shouted and struck with the whip. The Mule couldn't understand the raging shouts and screams, but they were the last sounds she ever heard.

CURT MOELLER

IX. The Frog and the Scorpion

One day a scorpion was waiting by the side of a small pond, when a frog came along and was about to enter the water.

"Excuse me, Frog, but I was wondering if you could help me. I want to go to the other side, but I can't swim, and the water is too wide for me to walk around. Would you ferry me across on your back?"

"I'm sorry" said Frog, "but I don't think that would be a good idea. I'm not naïve, I know who you are, Scorpion. No Frog ever had a happy ending from any dealings with a Scorpion. Your stinger is sharp, and my skin is very thin."

"Indeed" said Scorpion, "I know you're not naïve. Frogs are known amongst Scorpions as clever creatures, and so I would never try and trick you. I need to cross the water, and you are a great swimmer while I can't swim at all. If you are kind enough to ferry me across, you can be certain that I won't sting you, because if you were to die, then I would surely drown."

"Since I was a tadpole I've heard the fable of the frog who gives a scorpion a ride across a pond, only for the scorpion to sting halfway across and they both die. In that story the scorpion says it stung because it had to, it was in its nature."

"Oh that's just a story," said the Scorpion, "and nobody learns anything from fables. There are all sorts of stories out there, most of them made up just to scare little children. I must say, this whole thing seems quite childish to me."

"That's true" said Frog, "but I still feel very uncomfortable about it."

"Frog, my life will be in your hands if you ferry me across. I will be entirely at your mercy. The only one who should worry is me. However, the kindness of Frogs is legendary, and so I will trust you to take me safely across."

Frog was silent for a few moments, then took a few small steps to the edge of the water and waited. "Well, I suppose it is silly and cowardly of me to refuse. It is a really old story, from so long ago, and shouldn't mean anything to us. I know that I've never actually seen a scorpion do that. Very well, climb onto my back and I will swim across for you."

"Oh thank you Frog, you have no idea how much I appreciate it. I am really anxious to get to the other side of the water."

And so Scorpion climbed onto Frog's back, and

Frog began to swim slowly but steadily across the pond. When they reached the middle of the water, Frog could faintly hear Scorpion crying. "What is wrong?" Frog asked.

"I am so sorry Frog, but I am going to sting you. I can't help it. I can't resist the urge, it is simply in my nature. Now we will both die. I am so sorry Frog, I truly am."

"It is OK" said Frog, as he felt the Scorpion's stinger pierce his back. "Even before we left I knew that you would do it."

"What?! But now we are both doomed. Frog, if you knew the whole time that it was in my nature to sting you, why would you agree to ferry me across?"

"Because you asked. It is also in my nature."

X. The Crow and the Hummingbird

During a drought a Crow went in search of water, flying over the dry and dusty earth looking for ponds, streams, puddles, any kind of water at all, but seeing only the hard reddish-brown of a land that had almost forgotten what water was. The Crow also looked for signs of other animals drinking water, intent on taking that water from them if he could, for "thirst justifies any action" he thought to himself. He flew until his wings felt heavy, but he couldn't see any water anywhere, and he landed to rest on a patch of hard, baked earth.

The Crow saw a Hummingbird nearby that looked happy, healthy, well-fed, and completely unaffected by the drought. "Hello," said the Crow, feeling curious, suspicious, and just a little bit hopeful. It was hope born of two factors: firstly, the Hummingbird must have drank recently, so there might be water close by; and secondly the Crow was naturally much bigger and stronger than the Hummingbird, so he would have no trouble taking as much water as he wanted from the

Hummingbird. The Hummingbird ignored the Crow's greeting and flew over to a nearby tree, and hovered around it for a while. "Hello" the Crow said again, and this time the Hummingbird flew away.

The Crow stood on the hot earth trying to decide which way to fly off, his brain working slowly in the fierce dry heat. Before the Crow could choose which direction to go, the Hummingbird returned, and again flittered around the same tree. "Well, well," thought the Crow, "there must be something important at that tree," and he flew over to take a closer look.

The Crow watched the Hummingbird for a while, and eventually saw what he had hoped to see: the Hummingbird drinking water. There was an earthen vessel on the ground, in the shade beneath the tree, and the Hummingbird was dipping his long beak in, and very clearly taking sips. "Hello," the Crow said with a smile, "what do you have there?" The Hummingbird quickly flitted away to the other side of the tree, her wings making a buzzing-hum sound as she hovered there.

"Well, well, yes indeed, thank you, I don't mind if I do," the Crow said as he strutted up next to the earthen vessel with water inside. The Crow poked his beak around the hole for a while trying to figure out how to take a drink, but his beak wasn't long enough to reach the bottom of the vessel. The Crow flapped his wings to try and float above the vessel like the Hummingbird had done, but that isn't the way that a Crow flies, and he ended up banging into the tree a few times before crashing down on top of the vessel. The Hummingbird watched all of this from a distance, circling the tree, making a humming sound with her wings.

The Crow was angry and frustrated, but more than anything he was thirsty. He tried again and again to reach his beak far enough into the vessel, and each time he got close, but never close enough to get a drink of the precious water. The Crow knew that he couldn't continue like this forever; he needed water and a new approach to getting it. So, the Crow flew up to the highest branch of the tree, and sat there. The Hummingbird watched the Crow, and circled the tree, but never came very close to the Crow, who sat motionless. Eventually the Hummingbird flew to the vessel, hovered over it, placed her long beak inside, and drank. The Crow watched from above, and heard the Hummingbird's wings make their whining hum of a sound, and to him it sounded like laughter. "Ha, ha, ha, we shall see who laughs next little bird." The Crow leapt from the branch and quickly descended to the ground, but the Hummingbird saw his shadow move, and made her escape.

"Thanks for the lesson," the Crow said, more to himself than to the Hummingbird on the other side of the tree. The Crow tried his absolute best to copy the way that the Hummingbird drank water from the vessel, but his beak wasn't as long and he couldn't quite reach the water. As he tried to drink again and again, the Crow listened to the Hummingbird's wings, and heard it as laughter. He was angrier and thirstier than he had ever been, and being laughed at filled him with determination to continue trying, but always to no avail. The tired and thirsty Crow flew back up to the top branch of the tree and sat there.

After some time with the Crow not moving, the Hummingbird returned to the earthen vessel, hovered over it and took another drink while the Crow watched. "Even with her beak in the water she can still laugh at me!" thought the Crow, "we all fight for water, but it's a rule of nature that we don't delight in droughts and suffering. What evil creature is this who mocks me so endlessly? What horrible little bird is this that exists only to tease, and to infuriate? If I die, you will die with me evil tormentor!" The Crow threw his tired body from the top branch and hurtled downward with his talons pointed at the Hummingbird, but she was feeling fresh and healthy and easily avoided his claws. The Crow squawked and screamed at the

Hummingbird, cursing her hated laughter, and he used his beak to attack the neck of the vessel with ferocious zeal. Eventually the Crow collapsed beneath the tree, his beak broken and his feathers wet with his own blood, as the Hummingbird floated about, her wings beating out a humming sound that really doesn't sound anything like laughter.

XI. The Clever Cockroach

There was a group of Cockroaches living together in a colony. They scavenged food when they could get it, they bred, and they worked. The lives of Cockroaches can be meager at the best of times, but the community managed to survive in its own chaotic and haphazard way, and for many generations if it didn't flourish, it did at least persist.

One generation a very special Cockroach was born, and quickly earned the name the Clever Cockroach, for he was exceptionally bright, and his intellect was obvious from a very young age. The Clever Cockroach could find food faster than any other cockroach, and the Roaches all marveled at how he knew the fastest routes to reach food, and the best ways to take heavier bits of food back to the nest. The Clever Cockroach taught the Roaches his ideas and strategies as best he could, but their intellect was so far below his the best he could achieve were some improvements in the Roaches' techniques. The Roaches noticed that their lot was improving, and they were grateful for it.

The Clever Cockroach began going out to search for food less often, and instead stayed in the nest directing the Roaches, figuring that this was the best way to maximize the impact his intelligence could have on the well-being of the community. Soon the nest hummed with ordered activity, as opposed to the chaotic din of the past. Food was more plentiful, fewer Roaches were killed in traps or by predators, and the greater efficiencies meant that the time needed for labour was less, and for the first time ever Roaches had free time.

As the Clever Cockroach orchestrated the labour of the nest, he had the strongest and most skilled workers build him a large chair elevated on a dais, in the airiest corner of the nest close to the food storage. Proximity to food was determined to be a matter of efficiency, since the Clever Cockroach ate constantly while directing the Roaches, and had grown quite large. In fact, he grew so large that he couldn't easily leave his chair, so he sat and directed others, while dedicated servants brought him food in an endless procession.

The Clever Cockroach also reasoned that, since he was so superior to the Roaches, it was in the best interests of the community if future generations were able to share in his intellect. He decreed that henceforth only he would mate with the females of the community. However upsetting this decree was for the male Roaches, for the females it was exceedingly worse, as the Clever Cockroach had grown to a size and shape that barely resembled their species, and even worse, it was rumoured that he was vicious during mating.

The Roaches did not have much leisure time, but the efficiencies brought about by the recent innovations now afforded them a small amount of free time, and one day they used it to have a gathering outside the nest. They spoke of how unhappy they were, and of the Clever Cockroach's arrogance and abuse. Tension had slowly been growing over time and had reached a peak, and so the meeting attendees quickly became agitated. One of their number mentioned how they did have food in greater abundance now, but he was shouted down before anyone heard him. They decided to overthrow the Clever Cockroach and remove him from his throne. They stormed into the nest ready to attack, but were met with a wall of guards. The Clever Cockroach had anticipated the attack, and had created a cadre of guards from the Roaches, selecting those that he could most easily control and manipulate.

With a security team in place, the Clever Cockroach could have continued with the same life, King of the Roaches, with an endless supply of food and concubines, but one day his keen intellect saw a new opportunity. The anger of the Roaches continued and was plain to see, and in it the Clever Cockroach saw a chance to harness the energy of that anger to a serve a greater purpose. He began his most ambitious project yet, using the labour of all the Roaches for his task. His vision was grand and the project was of enormous magnitude, and he knew he couldn't explain it to the Roaches, but when they saw it they would understand, and they would know that the work had been for their own good.

The Clever Cockroach now flaunted the deeds that incensed the Roaches, gorging on food and copulating continuously in plain sight, spurring their anger so that their rage would translate to strength and energy for their work. Hours were extended and free time was now taken up. Every moment of every day was spent in the service of the great project, which steadily grew larger and larger, but still wasn't close enough to completion to give a hint as to its final shape. A few of the Roaches died of exhaustion during their labours, but the Clever Cockroach knew that the price of a few lives was small compared to the benefits of the great project. Soon all would be elevated, soon all would be great.

Ironically, it was one of the Clever Cockroaches guards that cut his head off. When the guard caught a hard-working Roach that collapsed and fell dead into his arms, he was overcome with emotions, his heart brimming over with fury, with guilt, with regret. He quickly and neatly cut off the head of the Clever Cockroach, who then stood up from his throne for the first time in a long while. Headless and in great pain he tried to speak to the Roaches, and explain the vision behind the great project. But being headless meant he lacked a mouth to speak, and so he began to thrash his limbs about in frustration, swinging furiously and randomly. He was ripped into innumerable pieces by all of the Roaches, and they ate every last bit of him.

XII. The Blind Cat and the Starlings

There was an orchard full of fruit trees, and a group of Starlings was drawn there, feeding on the insects that were there to feed on the fruit. The orchard had many fruit trees, aligned and keeping their order even as they ascended and descended the rolling hills. The trees were often watched over by two-legged creatures, who didn't stop the Starlings from feeding there, but did destroy any attempts to build nests. So, the Starlings visited the orchard daily to feed on the abundant insects and flew home to their nests at the end of the day. A great number of other animals passed through the orchard each day, so the Starlings kept their vigilance, and warned each other if a threat seemed near.

One animal who never bothered the Starlings was a cat that lived with the two-legged creatures. Everyone called her the Blind Cat, and although she wasn't fully sightless, it was true that she couldn't see at all out of one of her eyes, and only partially out of another. The Blind Cat was quite old, and walked with the type of limp that made it impossible to tell which of her four legs was the injured one, and gave the impression that perhaps it was all four. She always listened and smelled carefully for other animals and tried to avoid them, but sometimes was chased or harassed by visitors to the orchard who found it easy to creep up on her. She always survived the attacks, even if only because the two-legged creatures protected her for some reason. The Starlings watched all of the visitors to the orchard carefully, except the Blind Cat who seemed occupied with simply keeping herself alive.

One day the Starlings noticed that there were a lot less animals in the orchard. They nervously twittered and chirped and squawked as they discussed what was happening, as most animals fear change, especially change they can't understand. The Starlings agreed to investigate, and they flew in different directions to survey the area.

When they returned and discussed what they had seen, they determined that the two-legged creatures had built a long wall around the orchard, and this structure kept out almost all of the creatures that didn't fly. They decided that the construction must have taken some time, but the Starlings hadn't even noticed it because they were birds, so the structure around the orchard was of no consequence to them. The Starlings laughed together, and resumed their hunt for insects.

After some time, the Starlings realized that the wall encircling the orchard, the thing they hadn't even noticed for so long, had in fact brought them a benefit: there were no predators for the Starlings to worry about. The wall around the orchard kept out the foxes, it kept out the raccoons, it kept out the possums, and it kept out most other predators as well. It is true that other birds could also fly into the orchard, and some of those birds were much bigger and stronger than the Starlings, but Starlings are renowned for their speed and agility in the air, which makes them almost impossible to catch. And so, the Starlings feasted upon the insects of the orchard with a new sense of calm and ease.

The Blind Cat of course also noticed that there were so many fewer animals in the orchard, and she took the opportunity to explore the orchard. The Starlings didn't fear the Blind Cat, but they were still birds and she was still a cat, so they flew away when she got too close.

Life was very different after the wall went up, seeming like a new world with a new order, and the Starlings felt like masters of this new domain. The Blind Cat also enjoyed the lack of danger, and spent long hours sprawled in the sun, and the only time she moved was to leave the shade to follow the sun's rays, or to escape those rays in the shade, depending on her mood. The Starlings noticed this, and in amusement referred to it as The Shadow Dance. Life went on like this for a long time, and eventually the Starlings and the Blind Cat paid each other no attention at all.

One day The Shadow Dance brought the Blind Cat directly beneath the branches of the tree the Starlings were in, but they had long since stopped finding any amusement in the Shadow Dance, and paid no mind at all to the Blind Cat. One of the Starlings jumped down from a branch to pluck a small insect from the grass beneath the tree. The Starling snatched it up, and took a few steps towards another insect nearby. The Starling leapt forward to take the insect, bringing the mandibles of its beak together in a fatal snap. The Starling was on the side of the Blind Cat's good eye, and that little bit of vision and sound of the beak closing was enough to guide the Blind Cat, and she successfully caught her first Starling in many, many years.

CURT MOELLER

XIII. The Rose and the Carnation

Two flowers grew side by side, from young seedlings into tall flowers, and they spent each day together enjoying each other's company, and the feeling of the sunshine as it bathed them in warm light. The Carnation was a lovely pink hue, and the Rose was a beautiful scarlet red.

The Carnation wondered at the Rose's beauty, and often gazed longingly at her companion. Each day she complimented the Rose's beauty, and each day the Rose said thank you and you are a beautiful flower as well. Over time the Rose's beauty came to be almost everything the Carnation ever spoke about.

One warm late summer day the Carnation said: "Oh, how I long to be as beautiful as you are."

The Rose smiled and said: "we are both beautiful flowers. We should enjoy our sunshine and our time." The Carnation didn't like this answer, and thought the Rose was being dismissive.

The next day the Carnation again said "oh how breathtaking you are! So elegant and bold! Your beauty is beyond compare. How much I envy you my friend."

"It's just appearance, really," said the Rose, "you enjoy the sun's rays on your face every bit as much as I do."

The next day the Carnation again started to discuss beauty. "I don't have the petals that you have. My posture isn't as straight as yours, I mean, just look how straight you stand! I could never do that! Ohh, I'm so jealous. I wish I looked like you."

"I don't mean to be rude," said the Rose, "but I really don't have time to keep listening to this. You know that I think you're a beautiful flower. We miss our chance to enjoy the sun's rays if we chatter over these unimportant matters."

"Unimportant?" thought the Carnation. "It's unimportant to you who is so beautiful, but what about me? You have no idea how important it is to me." The Carnation had an urge to say these things aloud, but she restrained herself. Her resentment for the Rose grew, and she began to wonder what she could do to undermine the Rose. Could she shade her from the sun? Could she strangle her roots? Could she entice one of the animals to… The Carnation noticed something for the very first time: the Rose had a large dark blemish on the underside of one of her petals.

The next day, and the day after that, the Carnation

watched as the blemish grew, and another blemish formed. It was still late summer, and the nights hadn't yet turned so very cold, but already the end was clearly visible for the Rose.

"Oh my friend," said the Carnation, "you are starting to decay."

"Yes," said the Rose, "I can feel it. My time now will be very little. But still there is time to sit quietly and enjoy the sun's rays on my face."

The Carnation felt sorry for her friend's condition, and how quickly she was deteriorating, but she also took a small pleasure, that she tried to keep buried deep down in her heart, at seeing the Rose decay. The Carnation and the Rose sat together in those final days enjoying the warmth and light of the sun's rays, mostly in silence, although the Carnation still spoke glowingly from time to time of the Rose's former beauty.

XIV. The Moon

The Moon had a few friends and acquaintances among those that are awake at night; such as bats, leopards, cockroaches, and mice. But the Moon was a bit of a solitary figure, prone to dreaming and imagining, and generally kept to her quiet and contemplative self. She spent most of her time up in the sky, her perfectly round form glowing and gently illuminating the earth below. She led a simple, regimented life, raising her cool light up into the sky at the same time every day, and bringing it down again at the same time. Her only truly close friend was the Owl. They kept occasional company, when the two of them would sit on high quietly for hours, contemplating the world around them.

One day the Moon asked the Owl about the daytime. "I have heard that there are a lot more animals around during the day. Is that true?"

"Why do you ask me? You know that when you go underground, I go to sleep" replied the Owl. "I'm here, but I'm not awake."

"I know," said the Moon, "but you always seem to know everything that is going on. I've heard it from other animals. Some of them are awake both in the day and the night. You talk to more animals than I do, so you must have heard the same things."

"I have heard many things in my time, some so impossible that they inevitably were true, others so likely that ended up being nothing but fables."

"Aren't you ever curious to see the other animals?" asked the Moon.

"Curious? I don't give it much thought," said the Owl. "The game that I hunt is out at night, the life that I live is at night, so it benefits me most to pay attention to the nighttime. But yes, everyone says that it is much more crowded during the day, and there are more animals around. I believe it, because you can see all of the tracks and the scat that they leave behind."

"It would be interesting to see," said the Moon. The Owl didn't answer and let the topic drift away on the silence and disappear into the night.

The next night, the Moon started talking about the daytime again. The Owl didn't speak about it too much, but the Moon brought the subject up again and again, and said she thought of visiting the daytime, which made the Owl worried. "My friend," said the Owl, "we need your light to see. When we look up in the sky, the glow from your perfectly round body fills the world with the light we need. In the daytime they have someone called the Sun, and he lights up the world. In the nighttime we need you, we need your light to see and to live our lives."

"I know," said the Moon, "and I wouldn't ever do anything to hurt the nighttime. I just can't stop wondering about what goes on all day." The Moon and the Owl sat together for the rest of the night in silence, the Moon imagining the day, the Owl imagining what would happen if the Moon went away.

The Owl was always very appreciative of the light the moon provided, which was enough for the Owl to hunt, build a nest, watch for predators, and to live a contented life. The Moon provided light for all of the creatures of the nighttime, but to no benefit to herself: the Moon had only ever given, and had never asked for anything in return. The Owl wanted his friend to be happy, and he wanted to show his appreciation, so finally one day he said to the Moon "I think I can help you."

The Owl didn't need to say what he could help with, the Moon knew right away. "Oh please, tell me how!"

"Well," said the Owl, "we need to figure out how to light up the sky without you. You will sleep through the night, and then come out in the morning at the beginning of the day."

"I can lend you my light," said the Moon. "It would be heavy for you to lift alone for a long time, but perhaps a few other owls can take turns too? Would you be willing to do that for me?" The Owl was indeed willing, but first he needed to test that he was even able to lift the Moon's light. He gave it a try, and struggled mightily with the weight, but he was able to fly the light high up into the sky.

"Yes my friend, I am quite certain that I can get a few other owls to take turns, and we will keep the sky lit while you sleep and prepare yourself for the day. But I must say that I am worried for you. The day is for the majority, but our souls were made for the nighttime."

The next night, the Moon gave her light to the Owl, who had a few friends nearby to help. "Take this, it isn't hot. Hold it aloft for as long as each of you can in your turns. I know it is a heavy burden for an owl to carry, and I thank you my friends for your help." The group of owls said nothing in reply, for it wasn't for the Moon to thank them; they and the other nighttime creatures owed a debt of gratitude to the Moon. The Moon went to rest and anticipate the day, and the owls did a competent job of giving the night sky its faint glow of light (although, admittedly, some of the nocturnal creatures did wonder why the Moon was bobbing up and down in the sky so much that particular night, and why the light was smaller and less round than usual, but the light was sufficient for all of the creatures to go about their lives as usual).

The Moon tried to sleep, but was too anxious. She thought about the coming day, about the owls and their willingness to help, and about all of the hidden wonders she was soon to discover. She waited and waited, but never fell asleep, and in fact became more awake with each passing moment. Usually the Moon went to sleep when she could see the other light coming from over the horizon. This time, however, she didn't sleep, but waited with her eyes wide open. As the light grew a bit brighter, and the morning was coming into being, the Moon climbed high into the sky to look at the world.

The first thing she noticed was all of the birds. Not only were there so many of them, but they sang the most beautiful songs. "I've never heard a lovelier sound!" said the Moon. "And the flowers! Why, some new ones are opening up to face the Sun, one's that I've never seen before! Do you hide your pretty faces from me at night?" the Moon laughed. She watched the small creatures, taking their first tentative steps out of their homes before sprinting about hither and thither. She saw the dogs barking ceaselessly at everything that passed them. She saw the cows mooing and farting in the fields, sending a stench of sound and smell towards her. She saw the great elephants, with their piercing cries; the ducks and the swans playing a screeching call-and-response; the myriad insects buzzing randomly; the pleading bleats of goats that seemed to fear silence.

The Moon watched the busy daytime world, but her eyes hurt. She had never before seen a light so bright, so inescapable; it seemed to light up not only the surface of things, but their very core, and she felt that she was burning from the inside out. She tried to watch the animals, but the brightness of the light made it difficult to focus her eyes, and the cacophony of sounds made it difficult to focus her mind. For one accustomed to silence and cool light to be placed in this burning bright hive of activity was too much, and the Moon collapsed.

It took a great effort, and more than one of them almost crashed, but the Owl and his friends were able to hold the Moon's light aloft in the sky for a second night, to allow her time to rest and recuperate from her ordeal. On the third night, she took her light back and resumed her old role, but she was never the same again. She suffered from extreme spasms that caused her spherical body to twist into crescent shapes, and sometimes to disappear altogether. Perhaps most strangely, even though the daytime world almost destroyed the Moon, she was never able to stop being curious, and even to this day she will occasionally creep into the sky during the daytime to catch a glimpse of the opposite world.

XV. The Ass and the Wolf

A young ass was grazing next to a river on the sweet first grass of spring. The water of the river was high and fast, swollen with the last of the melted snow. The Ass enjoyed the young vegetation of the new season and the warmth of the sunshine on her body. The Ass became relaxed, and by the time she noticed the predator approaching in stealth, she was trapped between the Wolf and the rapids of the river.

Instead of running away, the Ass pretended to have an injured leg, and hobbled about slowly and clumsily, and made no attempt to dash off as the Wolf drew closer. The Wolf was puzzled by this, and stopped stalking the Ass, stood up straight, and said "hello there!"

"Hello," said the Ass quietly.

"What's wrong with you? Are you injured?"

"Indeed I am," said the Ass.

"What is your injury?"

"I have a shard of rock wedged into my foot. It causes me such pain, and I can barely walk, never mind run. I haven't been able to find anyone strong enough to pull it out. It's in too deep," the Ass told him.

The Wolf paused and thought for a while. He had seen the Ass from a great distance, he had used great skill as a hunter to approach his prey, and now he had it. He had accomplished his task. And yet, the Wolf wasn't happy. He thought: "an ass isn't much of a chase or a challenge at the best of times, but this one is small, and has a bad leg. I'm not a buzzard, or a jackal, or a rat. I don't scavenge for food, I like to hunt. Hmmm, she mentioned not finding anyone strong enough to remove the rock from his foot. I'll show her the strength of a hunter. I'll fix her leg to set her free and later chase her down in the hunt!"

"I'll help you!" said the Wolf aloud.

"Pardon me?"

"I said, I'll help you" the Wolf repeated.

"Why, may I ask? I had assumed you were here to eat me."

"Oh no, I don't want to eat you," the Wolf lied. "I only eat the really small animals, they taste better. You don't have anything to worry about. I'll pull the rock out of your foot."

"Really? Do you think you can? I'd be most grateful. It's such an excruciating pain. But nobody has been strong enough to pull it out so far."

The Wolf laughed with ease and confidence, and said "you haven't met anyone as strong as I am, you'll see."

"That's very kind of you, I can't thank you enough."

"It's my pleasure," said the Wolf with a smile that looked and felt genuine.

The Wolf moved behind the Ass and bent down near her hind legs to remove the rock. The Wolf froze when he realized that the Ass had shifted his limp, and was now favoring a different leg. The Wolf had been duped! The Ass pretended to be hurt to create the situation: her back leg wasn't injured, it was ready to deliver a lethal blow!

The Wolf was directly in line with the Ass's powerful hind legs, but the Ass didn't move. The Wolf was frozen in place, not because of fear or shock; it was the clarity that comes with facing certain death that showed him how impossible it was to escape his current situation, and revealed exactly what parts of his character had allowed himself to be so easily tricked. Still the Ass didn't raise a leg or make any motion to kick. After what seemed like a great many moments, the Ass shook first one back leg and then the other (for she had forgotten where her limp was supposed to be) and said "wow, look at that. The rock finally just fell out on its own."

"What wonderful timing," said the Wolf, who now stood up straight and moved away from the Ass. "I hope your healthy legs take you far."

"Thanks again for helping."

"You are welcome, and I thank you as well."

The Ass trotted off, and the Wolf watched her for a moment before going in the opposite direction, and neither looked back at the other.

CURT MOELLER

XVI. The Monkeys, Part One

I t is said that monkeys have two young at each birth. The mother cradles and adores one, but generally neglects the other. As they grow, the coddled one is given lots of food, and the neglected one has to scavenge to survive. As the protected one reaches a certain age, it takes its place amongst the leaders of the group. The neglected one, in the instances when one does survive to adulthood, is allowed to stay in the group, although is always the last to feed and has to sleep on the lowest branches.

One day a mother gave birth to two young. She took them both to safety and nursed them. When she had chosen a favourite, she began to feed her more often, and cuddle and nurse and rock and caress her more. The less-favored monkey got less food and less attention, and when still a baby had to learn to find food, and safe places to hide from predators.

One day the two young monkeys were playing together, racing to see who was fastest to climb from the ground to the top of the tallest tree, and back to the ground again. The race wasn't even close, and the neglected monkey reached the uppermost branch and swung back to the ground again before the coddled monkey had even reached the middle. All of the monkeys in the group saw this and hissed, for the coddled monkey was being groomed to be part of the leadership of the troop. It wasn't good at all for one of their future peers to be beaten so badly, and so publicly. The mother watched this all and was furious. She towered over the neglected young monkey, in fact was more than double her size, and swatted her across the face with the power of a protective matriarch. The mother grabbed the coddled monkey and carried her up in a tree.

"Come close my little one, come close my little one," said the mother as she rocked the little, coddled monkey, pressing her tightly to her chest. "You're bigger than that other monkey, you're faster than that other monkey, you're smarter than that other monkey, you're stronger than that other monkey, you're..." She rocked back and forth fiercely, squeezing her young one tightly, shifting gaze erratically in every direction around her. She rocked and jabbered and looked about for quite some time before she realized that she had suffocated her young.

XVII. The Monkeys, Part Two

Two monkeys were born at one birthing, as was the norm. Very quickly, as monkeys are wont to do, the mother began to favour one and neglect the other. They lived like that as the two young monkeys grew; one adored and coddled, the other neglected and forced to learn to survive. According to some, one day the neglected monkey beat the favoured monkey in a fight, and beat her so badly she never recovered and passed away at a very young age. According to others, her own mother killed her for disobedience. Still others say that the child was sick and weak, and died of fright when she heard a hyena laugh.

As the neglected monkey grew older, she displayed not only great strength, speed, and agility, but also great cunning and intelligence. Many times she had been the first to warn the group of impending danger, or to guide the group to food and water sources during droughts. She behaved with such power and grace that it was the smoothest and most natural transition imaginable when she took leadership of the troop, despite her somewhat questionable background and her still youthful age. She was widely regarded as the best leader the troop had had in anyone's memory, and the group flourished in health and numbers.

Eventually the new leader came to the age when she too would mate, and she gave birth to two young. There is a custom amongst monkeys that a mother will favour one child over the other. The mother will give one everything it asks for and more, and the other barely anything. The leader, like all monkeys eventually do, chose her favourite. Her heart was brimming over with the sadness that always resides somewhere inside the strongest loves, as she pushed her favourite off the branch and picked up and coddled her less favourite, holding her young gently to her breast and staring off into the distance.

CURT MOELLER

XVIII. The Caged Birds

T he Birds were small but swift and nimble in flight, and of all the animals in the forest they probably lived the safest lives. It is true that from the ground the Cats always pursued them, and from above the Hawks tried to swoop down and snatch them, but the Birds were cautious and careful by nature, and remained alert without panic, and so were able to keep themselves safe.

One day the Birds were feeding on berries at the edge of the forest, near the den where the Foxes lived. "What beautiful voices you have!" said one of the Foxes.

"Why, thank you. It is a beautiful day, isn't it?" replied one of the Birds.

"Indeed it is, and made more beautiful by your melodies," another of the Foxes said, and several more echoed their agreement. The next day and the day after the Birds returned to the same area, to finish off whatever berries still clung to the bushes. Each day they bid the Foxes good morning, and then the Birds sang to each other as they flitted from branch to branch and ate the berries.

"Please come here every day to eat" said a Fox. "We enjoy the music very much."

"Thank you," replied a Bird, "but the berries are almost gone. We will fly off to find more tomorrow." The Foxes thought about this for a while. Of course it was reasonable for any animal to go in search of food, but they didn't want to lose the music that they had grown to enjoy so much.

"We will build homes for you, and bring you food to eat. We can find lots of berries, we'll bring you branches of them. In exchange, you agree to stay here and sing for us every day." The Birds laughed at this offer.

"We sing because we want to sing, if we were forced to do it our voices wouldn't sound as sweet. But even more than this, we are Birds, we value freedom most of all, to be stuck in one place would be horrible for us. This little piece of forest where you live is very nice, but for Birds a life without freedom is a life without joy." The Foxes said they understood and wished the Birds good luck.

Days later, the Birds were eating seeds from the ground in another part of the forest. Only two or three Birds ate at a time, while the others watched from branches in surrounding trees, and gave warning at any signs of danger. Even with so many watching eyes in the branches, a group of Cats got so close that a swipe of a claw stripped one of the Birds of a few feathers. They all quickly flew up to high branches for safety, and chattered nervously at the close escape. Neither the Cats nor the Birds noticed the Foxes watching from a distance.

The next day, the Birds were feeding on seeds again. After the previous day's scare they kept even greater numbers in the trees to keep watch for the Cats. Knowing that there were still a great many seeds on the ground, the Foxes calculated that the Birds would return again that day, and they guided the Hawks to that same place. The Hawks thanked the Foxes, and then climbed to a great height in the sky, and bore down on the Birds with fierce speed and pointed talons. The Birds in the highest branches noticed the shadows pass over them, and they called out warnings as they flew to lower branches for safety. The Foxes ran to the trees and growled and jumped at the Hawks that flew low, and eventually all of the Hawks flew away.

None of the Birds was caught by the Hawks, and even though none had really even been that close to being caught, the Foxes began to say things like "oh my, that was a close one," and "more than one Bird was almost snatched," and "are we even sure all the Birds are still here?" The Birds felt nervous and anxious after being attacked in the same place two days in a row, and thanked the Foxes for their help.

"We're very happy to help," said one of the Foxes, "it's unfortunate we can't always be near you to keep you safe." The Birds thanked them again, and flew off to rest after their ordeals.

The next day, the Foxes went to the opposite side of the forest, as far as it was possible to go from the place where the Birds had been attacked by the Cats and the Hawks. As they expected, they soon heard the music of the Birds singing. One of the Foxes crept stealthily beneath a bush, and shook it and made loud noises. This scared the Birds, who immediately stopped singing and flew up into high branches. The rest of the Foxes then walked slowly beneath the tress, pretending not to notice the Birds, and spoke in rather loud voices about "the Cat-Hawk Conspiracy."

"Hello friends!" the Birds called down to the Foxes. "Look up here!"

"Oh hello," replied one of the Foxes, "why don't you come down and chat with us?"

"Sorry, but we heard something moving around down there, we're not so sure it's safe."

"Fear not when you are with us. You are our friends, and we make sure you are protected." The Birds quickly chatted amongst themselves and agreed that it did seem safe to go down to the ground with the Foxes there, so they flew down.

"We heard you talking. Did you say something about the Cats and the Hawks?" one of the nervous Birds asked.

"You haven't heard of the Cat-Hawk Conspiracy? It's the talk of the forest. The Cats and the Hawks are disappointed that they missed out on catching you, and they decided to join forces. From now on they will attack you from the top and the bottom, and from every direction, and all at once. We're sorry to have bad news to share, but it doesn't look good for you Birds."

The Birds twittered and tweeted in such a flurry that the Foxes couldn't understand a word that was said, but they didn't need to, it was enough to see the fear. "Do not worry, "said one of the Foxes, "we will stay with you for the rest of the day and make sure you are safe." The Birds thanked the Foxes profusely, and then returned to their cacophony of tweets to discuss their predicament. The Foxes were true to their word, and stayed with the Birds until the end of the day.

Very early the next morning, when the Foxes were just emerging from their den, the Birds came to visit. "Good morning friends!" they called to the Foxes, who responded in kind. "We have come to ask a favour, and we hope you will receive our request gladly."

"What might that favour be?" asked a Fox.

"Many days ago, you had offered to house us and feed us, in exchange for our song. We're afraid that perhaps we were a bit too hasty when we said no. Living here in this one place would be giving up some of our freedom, but we would also be in the company of you Foxes, our new friends. You can keep us safe from the Cat-Hawk Conspiracy, for while there is little joy in a life without freedom, there is no joy in a life without life!"

"Well, we do enjoy your music, and we have already built houses for you to use, so it does seem like the most natural thing in the world for you to come and live with us. Look, some of us are bringing the houses over to you now. They are made from branches and grass, the materials most comfortable for Birds."

"They are indeed beautiful houses, and we thank our friends the Foxes. But may we ask, why are there doors and locks on the houses?"

"Oh, those are there for you if you choose to use them. They are your houses." The Birds chatted amongst themselves and quickly decided that this was a nice thing for the Foxes to provide for them, even though they would never use the doors or locks.

"Thank you," said the Birds, "we know we can live

safely here. We can still fly from house to house and enjoy some freedom. We will be happy with the fact that we are alive, and that will give joy to our songs, and our songs will give joy to you."

For several days the Birds and the Foxes lived like this: the Birds stayed in or near their houses and sang most of the time, and the Foxes ventured out to get food for themselves and berries for the grateful birds, always with a few Foxes staying behind to guard the area around their den. The Birds had fewer berries and less variety than they used to have, but the Foxes told them about the lack of berries throughout the entire forest, and how lucky they were to have any berries at all. The Birds agreed that they were indeed very lucky, and they thanked the Foxes again.

One day all of the Foxes went out for food and berries, leaving none behind on guard. A short while after the Foxes left, the Birds noticed the Cats slowly encircling their houses, and began warning each other of the danger.

"Let's fly up!" a few of the Birds said.

"No, don't! The Hawks must be with them," others said. "It's a trap! Go into your houses and close the doors!"

The Foxes soon returned and chased away the Cats. They found the Birds all still alive and in their houses. "Are you alright friends?"

"Yes, we're all alive. We're so happy you returned. The doors on the houses you built helped us, but the Cats would have soon had them opened. We don't know what would have happened if you had returned a moment later."

"Well, we are glad that the doors were a help to you. Now you know that you can fly up into your houses and close the doors anytime you need to be safe."

"It wasn't that easy," said the Birds. "Our wings aren't made for opening and closing doors. We were slow, and the Cats almost got us. And then the Cats were trying to open the doors, and they almost succeeded. The doors helped, but we can't operate the locks. If they come back with the Hawks, I don't think we would survive."

"The doors are sturdy, and even without the locks we think you will be alright. Of course, the talons of Hawks are very good at opening doors, but still, we are sure you will be fine. And besides, in the rare chance that one Bird is caught, all of the Hawks and the Cats will focus on ripping a piece of flesh off that Bird to eat, and will ignore the rest of you."

"But, wouldn't we be safer with the doors closed and locked?" asked one of the Birds.

"Safer, yes of course," answered the Foxes, "but with less freedom. We want you to be safe, and we want to enjoy your music every day, but we don't want to you to lose your freedom. You yourselves said that without freedom your songs wouldn't be as sweet."

"But we are so scared, dear Foxes. Now our voices only tremble with fear. If you protect us and keep us safe, our voices will overflow with sweetness, and we will sing beautiful songs for you whenever you command."

"Well," the Foxes said, "we could keep you inside the houses with the doors closed. But we wouldn't dream of keeping the doors locked…:unless of course you insist…"

CURT MOELLER

www.ingramcontent.com/pod-product-compliance
Lightning Source LLC
Chambersburg PA
CBHW020630130626
46552CB00003B/1164